All kinds

Who cares about race and colour?

illustrated by **Pam Adams**

Published by Child's Play (International) Ltd

© M. Twinn 1989   ISBN 0-85953-363-8 (hard cover)   Printed in Singapore

ISBN 0-85953-353-0 (soft cover)

It takes all kinds to make a world.

caucasoid   *mongoloid*

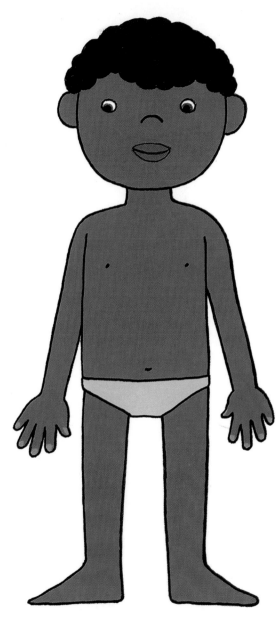

negroid

Look at these three boys.
What differences can you see ?

Look at the colour of their skin.

What about their eyes ?
What about their hair ?
Can you see other differences ?

These are differences of race.

Race simply means a family
or a group of related people
from the same part of the world
and all their descendants.

There are three basic racial
types: mongoloid, negroid and
caucasoid. We often distinguish
these groups by skin colour:
yellow, black, white. Most people
in Asia are mongoloid;
most people in Africa are negroid;
most people in Europe
are caucasoid.

But all people belong to the human
race. It's like one big family.

Thousands of years ago, each race lived

People rarely
saw anyone
from another
race.

Travel
was slow.

in a different part of the world.

Strangers were sometimes welcomed,
particularly if they came to trade.

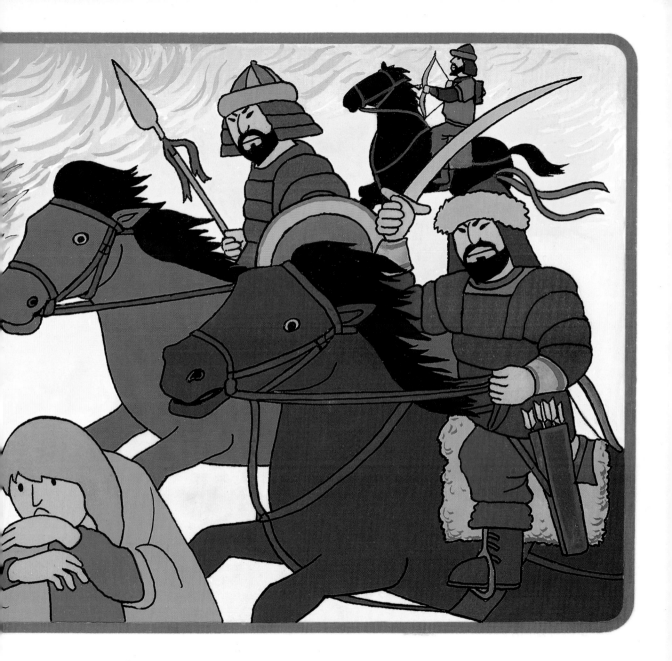

But often they came to steal or conquer.

Defeated people were often carried away as slaves.

Travellers brought back fantastic stories,
which made people afraid of strangers.

Today, travel is fast.
We visit faraway places just for pleasure.

Or we go to live in another country to find work.

Today, there are people of every race and colour

in every walk of life . . .

There is no reason why people of different races
should not work or play together happily.

Wherever we come from, whatever we look like,
we all belong equally to the society we live in.

Race and colour have nothing to do with being good or bad.

**Race and colour
have nothing to do
with being kind or mean,
fast or slow,
strong or weak,
clever or stupid.**

It is difficult being in a strange place,

especially if you don't speak the language.

It is even worse, if people make fun of you.

So, we should always try to make newcomers
feel at home and introduce them to our friends.

People from other countries bring variety

and excitement into our lives.

We enjoy new foods, music and styles of clothing.

But friendships and new ideas are the best things.

We can be proud of our own origins, but
we must respect the customs and traditions of others.

There is much we can learn from one another.
It's much more fun when we share.

When we are friends,
we don't notice race and colour.